Saying Goodbye to Barkley

For Jay and Aaron who are my stars, my universe, my very own Big Bang. And for Jen and Anouska. Thank you for your support, encouragement, and belief that my ideas might be more than just ideas.
– D.S.

For Asher, my boy with a beautiful heart.
– N.J.

First published 2019
EK Books
an imprint of Exisle Publishing Pty Ltd
PO Box 864, Chatswood, NSW 2057, Australia
226 High Street, Dunedin, 9016, New Zealand
www.ekbooks.org

A CiP record for this book is available from the National Library of Australia.

ISBN 978-1-925335-96-5

Designed by Big Cat Design
Typeset in Minya Nouvelle 18 on 28pt
Printed in China

This book uses paper sourced under ISO 14001 guidelines from well-managed forests and other controlled sources.

10 9 8 7 6 5 4 3 2 1

Saying Goodbye
to
Barkley

Devon Sillett

Nicky Johnston

Super Olivia and her amazing sidekick
Barkley did everything together.

Good deeds.

Sniffing out clues.

Catching the bad guys!

One was never without the other.

They were a perfect pair.

But then ...

Mama sat Olivia down to explain that even sidekicks need to retire at some point.

Olivia said she understood. But really, she
didn't. After all, Super Olivia and the Amazing
Barkley were two pieces of a puzzle. One
without the other just wasn't complete!

Still, Super Olivia did her best to keep up the fight against crime. She put on her cape and mask. She went through the motions.

But it wasn't the same.

And the bad guys kept getting away with it.

Olivia didn't have the heart
to be Super anymore.

And then, just like that, Barkley was gone.

Olivia was too sad to eat.
She felt too sad to sleep.

She dreaded dreaming every
night because she'd wake up and
Barkley would be gone again.

But at least when she was
dreaming, she got to spend a little
more time with her best friend.

'I'm so sorry, Sweetie,' her mother told her. 'I know it hurts, but you have to get on with things eventually.'

Olivia didn't want to
get on with things.

How could she?
A superhero needs
her sidekick.

A sidekick that she could only see when she closed her eyes was not much help in fighting crime and catching the bad guys.

But then ...

Olivia thought about the fun they had together. She realized that Barkley wouldn't want her to stop doing good deeds and catching bad guys, no matter what.

She had an idea.

For the first time in a while, Olivia rolled over and slept soundly.
When she woke up, she jumped out of bed to tell Mama her plan.

Mama wasn't sure at first.

'It won't replace Barkley, you know,' she said.

'I know Mama. Nothing ever will.
But Barkley loved rescuing people.
Why not rescue animals too?'

That afternoon, they spent a
long time at the shelter. There
were so many to choose from,
and each needed a loving home.

Eventually, Olivia settled on a big,
white fluffy thing named Spud.
Olivia couldn't wait to teach her
how to catch the bad guys!

As it turned out, Spud
was a terrible sidekick.

She was rotten at fighting crime.
And she couldn't care less about
catching the bad guys.

Spud was no Barkley.

And Olivia still missed
Barkley deeply.

But Spud was Spud, and Olivia
grew to love her very much.

Best of all, Olivia knew that Barkley would be very proud of Olivia for rescuing Spud, even if she was a useless sidekick. Because Spud was something different entirely.

A lovable lump.

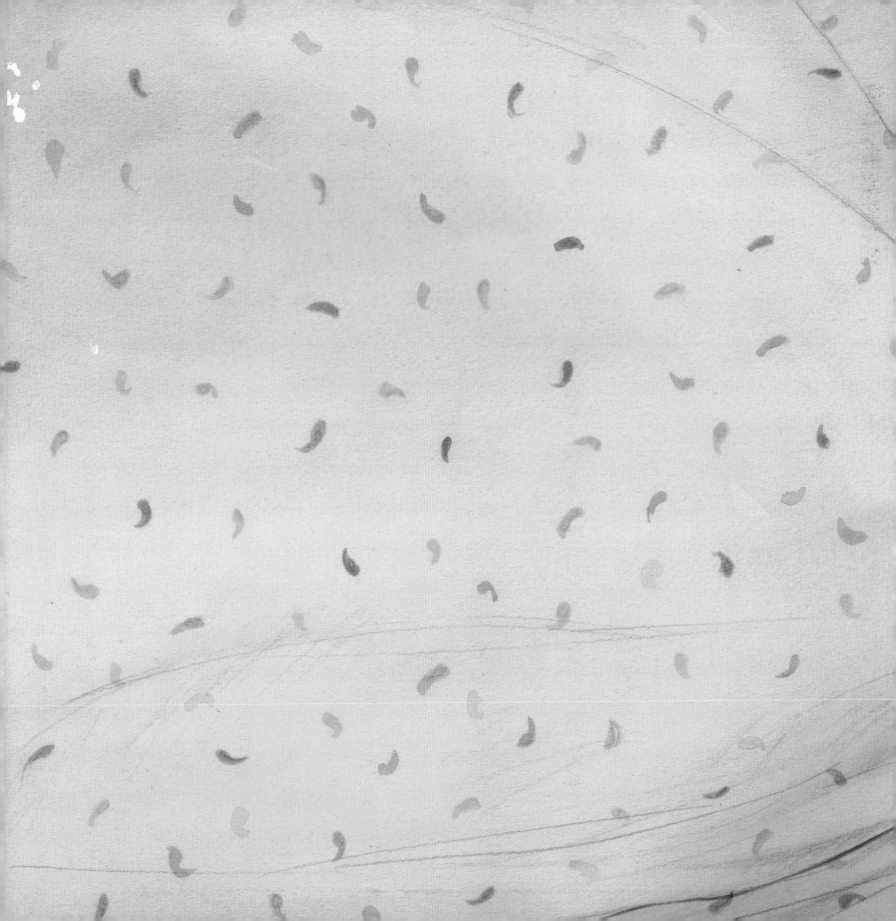